P.S. Charlie

"Memoirs of a Little Brave Girl with a Big Brave Heart"

Part 1

By

Tommia Brookins

Acknowledgments

Special Appreciation and Thanks To…

My Editor and my right hand, *Holly Hampton*

My Illustrator, Thank you for bringing Charlie to life, *Brandon Treadway*

My Husband, Thank you for your infinite love and support

My Sisters, Thank you for your constant inspiration

My Mother, Thank you for always believing in me and teaching me to always believe in myself

Team Brave Heart, *Without you guys, there would be no me*

"This book is dedicated to all of my brave hearts all over the world; the ones who have discovered their bravery within and also the ones who are still searching. NEVER stop searching, just look deep into your heart and that's where you'll find your hidden bravery. I would also like to dedicate this book to my mom. She is the reason I discovered my inner brave girl. I love you."

-Tommia B.

Copyright 2016 by Tommia Brookins
Published by
Brookins Publishing
Decatur, Ga. 30034
Printed in the United States of America – 2016 – First Edition
Library of Congress Publication Data ISBN 9780692654088

P.S. Charlie is a riveting tale of a little brave girl facing the scariest time in her life when she is diagnosed with a lifelong illness. What an awesome tool to help patients, young and old alike, face whatever challenge life has thrown at them. Taking a page from Charlie's journal, we can all find out that our hearts may be braver than we thought!
Andrea Reid
Board Certified Nurse Practitioner
Atlanta, GA

P.S. Charlie, is a delightful story that teaches her loved ones about courage and finding your happy place in the midst of uncertainty and fears. As a reader, I quickly found myself falling in love with Charlie and cheering for her recovery. In the end, I am sure that Charlie will not only teach young people about bravery, but she taught me a few things as well! This is a must read for any child and "child at heart." As a pediatrician, it's a book I would recommend for any patient needing to find their inner bravery.
Keyendria Kellogg Garth M.D.

P.S. Charlie is Sassy and real, like its author, but comfortable. It has the sassiness of its author, evidenced by Charlie's "smart mouth," and the realness of a horrible disease. However, it is comfortable enough that you actually enjoy reading a story about a young girl battling Lupus. Readers of all ages can appreciate Charlie's bravery and perseverance. No matter the disease, no matter the problem, no matter the age or size, this story teaches that a brave heart, faith, and family are awesome remedies. P.S. Charlie is inspiring! P.S. Charlie is Brave!
Shay Price Ed.S
Freshman Academy Principal

CONTENTS

PREFACE

Although I was very young, six years old I think, I remember that summer like it was yesterday. I felt weak on most days and could barely walk on other days. I was sleeping the summer away while all of the other kids were outside having fun. My parents were taking me back and forth between the pediatrician's office and the hospital only for me to be sent home with a different diagnosis and more medicine each time. Once it was pneumonia, another time the flu; one doctor even said that my flares were a result of me suffering from anxiety! The pains and aches in my joints only worsened until my mom had finally had enough! My parents researched and researched until they found the best pediatrician in Georgia. After a long series of tests, my parents were told that I had an incurable disease known as lupus. I was too young to understand how serious something like lupus was at the time, but I could tell that my family was having a rough time with the news; meanwhile, the pain I was in was giving me a rough time of my own. But that was only the beginning.

CHAPTER 1

"The Dreams"

Lulu the Unicorn and I galloped freely through the Candy Pepper Forest. The sweet smell of baked goodies and calla lilies filled the air. Bouncing gumballs and jumping pop rocks sprung through the forest whimsically. I could hear berries popping from the Strawberry Lemonade Fountain and the bittersweet drops of lemonade splashing to the ground, and some even into Lulu's mouth! I abruptly yanked Lulu's reins, stopping her in her tracks. "Lulu! A French toast tree! Over there!" I screamed in excitement.

"Charlie, we are approaching The Deep of the Candy Pepper Forest, which used to be forbidden. It is no longer forbidden, BUT no one enters the Deep. Thousands of years ago, many were known to enter the Deep, but they never came out."

"Oh come onnnn Lulu," I plead, "A FRENCH TOAST TREE? We can't pass this up! You know how much I LOVE French toast! What do you always tell me? 'All it takes is one little click of your hooves to start, and then you're well on your way!'"

Lulu is the bravest Unicorn in the Candy Pepper Forest; however, a reluctant tone filled Lulu's voice. I had never seen Lulu scared of anything before, so instead of relying on her to go first like I usually do, I proceeded toward the tree, hoping Lulu would follow closely behind.

As I got closer to the French toast tree, the sound of Lulu's clicking heels was slowly being drowned out by what sounded like ocean waves. I looked around, and to my surprise, I did not see an ocean anywhere. Unfortunately, I did not see Lulu either. At this point, I realized

I had officially crossed over into The Deep. I grew more and more nervous as I walked further into this unfamiliar land, wishing that Lulu had followed me. A light mist began to swarm around me and the crisp, clean air quickly turned into a dense, red fog. As I approached the French toast tree, all of my fears slipped away as I anticipated the sweet and savory taste of French toast melting in my mouth. Suddenly, the air grew hotter, and it wasn't long before I noticed that the red mist was no regular mist—it was breath! I immediately stopped in my tracks. I found that the sound I had been hearing was no ocean—it was the sound of a dragon breathing!

An enormous orange creature rose from the fog. I stood still, frightened to the core. The dragon had black stripes that started at the crest of its forehead, reaching all the way to his sharp, dagger-like tail. He had long horns, sharp toes and nails, and a green snout. The dragon's piercing, round eyes glared directly at me. I wanted to scream for Lulu, but I couldn't move.

I glanced to my right and then to my left where I saw a huge tarnished staff that looked like it had once belonged to a warrior. A warrior who had probably been defeated by this horrifying dragon. I had to get to it somehow. Treading lightly, I took one step toward the staff, and then another, and then one more. The dragon let out a loud roar. I had to move, NOW! I quickly jumped on top of the staff and grabbed it. *It's now or never!* I thought. I closed my eyes and charged toward the dragon! I found myself screaming as I used every ounce of my energy to thrust my arm forward and jab the dragon with the tarnished staff!

After the third jab, I stopped. *Is that laughter?* I thought to myself. I peeked through one eye to find that the dragon was laughing hysterically. *HE'S TICKLISH!* I didn't know if I should laugh with him, leave him alone, walk away, or continue to try bringing this terrifying creature down. Overwhelmed, I decided that I could use this opportunity to get away. I called for Lulu and watched as she slowly appeared through the fog. I climbed onto Lulu's back as quickly as I could and we made a swift escape!

Once we made it out of The Deep, Lulu asked, "Was he laughing?"

"Yes! Yes, Lulu!" I exclaimed, my heart still beating fiercely. "You should've seen how brave I was. I noticed a staff on the ground; I picked it up, ready to defeat him; and to my surprise, he bursts into laughter! If I never would've picked up that staff and tried to defeat the dragon, I would still be standing there with my eyes closed!" Suddenly I had a thought and quickly snatched Lulu's reins. She halted and I hastily jumped off of Lulu onto the ground.

Lulu shouted, "What is it Charlie? Another dragon? See any staffs?"

"No, no," I replied, shaking my head forcefully. "I just realized, I didn't even get my French toast!"

We both fell out laughing. I laughed so hard that my eyes begin to swell with tears. Finally, exhausted from laughing, I closed my eyes and lay on the ground, smiling and reminiscing on my recent act of bravery.

***

"All done Charlie," said a soft voice.

I opened my eyes, but I saw no calla lilies, no bouncing gumballs, no jumping pop rocks, no lemonade fountains, and no Lulu. Just the dialysis clinic, needles, and lupus. If only my dreams matched my reality. *Yep, back to reality*, I thought to myself.

I started having these dreams when I started dialysis, but I only have them during my treatments! Not that I look forward to my treatments, but the dreams provide a nice escape from real life and they have awakened something inside of me that I forgot ever existed. This is the side I thought I lost the day the doctor told me I had lupus. A more exciting, optimistic side of me! Before I was diagnosed, I was a worry free little girl without a care in the world. Now, I get worried if I get so much as a

scrape on my knee!

CHAPTER 2

"Being Different"

Dear Journal,

My awful scars apparently are only awful to me.

My mom says, "Charlie, you are the most beautiful girl in the world."

My sister says, "Charlie, your scars are just a sign of your bravery."

My daddy says, "It could be worse, baby girl."

My friends say, "But you don't even look sick, Charlie."

But when I look in the mirror, the same mirror I work so hard to avoid, all I can see staring back at me are scars. I have high hopes of one day becoming that beautiful, brave girl that everyone else sees, but for now, my scars are the only "brave" part of me.

Love Always,

Charlie

P.S. I know my scars are only a little part of me, but why does the ugliest *part have to be the part that everyone else sees first?*

***

When your parents know you won't be just any ordinary girl, they give you a boy's name. That's what my parents did with me. My name is Charlie. Charlie Bradshaw to be exact and I am no ordinary girl. I'm twelve-and-a-half years old and I'm in the seventh grade. I have one sister, Roberta, but everyone calls her Rocky. She hates her name because she thinks it's an old lady's name. Sometimes I call her Roberta just to make her angry. Rocky is fourteen years old and she's in the ninth grade, but she thinks she's a grown up because she wears perfume and dangly earrings. Rocky is the cooler sister, and she's more popular too. She doesn't rub it in my face, though. She's actually very supportive, and not just with me, but with our mom too.

Rocky and I live with our mom, but our dad picks us up on the weekends. He takes us to his house where he lives with his other family. His wife has two little boys and they are super annoying. I don't tell anyone that they're my stepbrothers because they're so embarrassing. One time, we went to dinner at a fancy Chinese restaurant, the kind where they cook the food in front of you, and one of them kept putting his hands in the fire on the grill. Afterwards, we had to go to the hospital and everything! It was the worst night ever.

Ever since my dad moved out, my mom has seemed kind of lonely. When I first noticed how lonely she seemed, I tried giving the mailman her number so that they could go on a date, but she just got mad at me. I got into so much trouble that I was grounded for an entire week! I guess that's what I get for trying to help.

We all live in Koala Lowlands, a small town in Georgia. I love growing up in Georgia. It never snows and everybody knows everybody, especially my mom. She always knows what everyone is doing, why they're doing it, and who they're doing it with. She and our nosy neighbor, Ms. Bittersnap, are the best of friends, probably because Ms. Bittersnap talks just as much as my mom does. Most of the kids in the neighborhood are scared of Ms. Bittersnap because she always smells like mothballs and collard greens. I'm not scared of her, but I don't get too close to her either.

Ms. Bittersnap sat on her front porch the entire summer and watched in disgust as kids ran up and down the street all day. Sometimes, she would chase after them and scream, "You little raga monsters need to stay out of the street before you get run over!" I would sit at the foot of my bed and snicker at the sight of kids running home in terror to their mommies.

Staring out of the window is what most of my summers consist of. I don't go outside much, especially in the summer. My skin can't handle the sun. If I'm in the sun for too long, I break out in these awful blisters and bright red bumps. My skin gets all itchy and tender, and I usually have to go to the hospital. My mom gets super emotional when my lupus flares up, so I do everything in my power to prevent it, even if that means I have to watch the summer go by from my window.

It took a while for me to accept that I couldn't play outside in the beautiful sun like all of the other kids, but I eventually got used to it. Now, I just find things to do that make me feel like I'm outside. I've found that having an imagination can take me very far. Sometimes, my imagination is so vivid that I can actually taste the honey in the honey suckle flowers; I can smell the foul odor from the pussy willows that overtake the fresh, flowery scent of a summer day; and I can hear the bumblebees buzzing from ear to ear. Once, I got so caught up in my imagination that I actually felt a bumblebee sting me! Ouch! My imagination hasn't always been this free though. I used to stay bottled up in my room, writing in my journal.

I've had lupus for about six years now. No one actually knows what causes it, but my mom always tells me that it's not my fault that I have it. The first thing kids ask me when they find out is "Is it contagious?" I always want to respond, "No, idiot!" but I usually just smile, shake my head, and walk away. Because of the lupus, my body isn't really able to fight germs like other people's bodies, so you can imagine why I keep to myself. My doctor is always telling me to try my best to stay away from germs and sick people—that means I have to stay away from like, everyone and everything in the world! I have to take medicine every day and every night—sometimes more than that if I'm all sore and achy. I'm not able to spend a lot of time in the sun or participate in sports; you know, outdoor activities. My mom lets me go outside and play with my sister when the sun starts to set. This makes the other children jealous, so it all works out, I guess.

Every day is not a bad day, though. Some days are really good and some are really bad. The sucky thing about lupus is that you never know what days will be good and what days will be bad. I can remember one particular night, I was playing the part of Annie in the school play. I was the youngest girl to ever play Annie's role at The Stafford School of the Arts, and the best, in my opinion. My entire family sat in the audience, puffed up like peacocks because they just knew I would be amazing!

When I entered the auditorium, I was amazed! It was one of the most beautiful sights that I had ever seen. The lights were captivating, the atmosphere was magical, and the music was majestic, but little did I know, those very lights would soon play a massive part in shaping the next year of my life. As I sang and danced, I could see my mom, dad, granny, and Ms. Bittersnap in the crowd singing along. The music was pounding and all of the parents were shouting their children's names.

Suddenly, I began to feel a tingling sensation on my face. I started to sweat uncontrollably and my heart was pounding. Every time I gazed into the lights, my eyes would burn fiercely. I knew that I had to get off of that stage and away from those lights, but I wanted to finish what I started, so I pushed through until the end of the show.

The next day, I felt worse. My face felt as if it was on fire! I attempted to ignore the pain, but as the day went on, the pain intensified. By noon, my previously pretty skin was covered with blisters. My throat was starting to close and I thought I was going to die.

My mom rushed me to the hospital, and by the time we got there, my face was so swollen that it felt like it was going to burst at any moment. The doctor kept pricking me with needles and I hate needles! You would think that I would have been used to them by then, but I cried like a little baby.

Although they gave me more popsicles and watermelon than I could imagine, being in the hospital is no fun. Every day consisted of doctors and nurses running in and out of my room, pricking me with needles, resulting in sleepless nights. The total opposite of fun! I was scared to sleep there alone, because I would have night terrors and wake up every night in cold sweats, so my mom stayed with me every night. My cousins and my best friend, Lizzy came to visit me almost every day. They brought games, movies, and playing cards, which made the days seem a little shorter.

It was all so unexpected and terrifying. When I was diagnosed with lupus, I knew that I had to avoid sunlight, but I didn't know that included stage lights. Over the course of two weeks, I ended up with thirty-two scars. It's been years since then, but I still have those scars today. My family is always telling me how pretty I am and pretend that the scars aren't

there, but I don't think anything can make up

for these scars that will never go away.

CHAPTER 3

"Rocky"

Dear Journal,

I miss you. It's been a while. Three months to be exact. Now that the summer is over, the sun is fading and September is peeking around the corner. The leaves are on their way down, the nice warm weather is shifting to another hemisphere, the ice cream trucks aren't running as frequently, the constant sound of laughter in the street is gone, the annoying car alarms and balls bouncing off of them is no more, and the swimming pool is covered. No more walking down the street in colorful swimsuits, flip-flops, and sunglasses in anticipation of that fresh chlorine smell. No more road trips to Granny's on the weekends just to get her freshly baked, warm and gooey chocolate chip cookies and freshly squeezed lemonade. One by one, the beautiful butterflies that I chased all summer have all departed, the lemonade stands have disappeared, and even the bumblebees have stopped buzzing around. I hate to admit this, but I'm going to miss the itchy mosquito bites and flies hovering over my plate when Daddy barbeques...

Love Always,

Charlie

P.S. I miss my daddy's barbeque.

***

"Charlie!"

I slammed my journal closed in frustration. I have to constantly remind my mom how much I hate it when she interrupts my writing time, but, in her defense, I'm always writing. I love my journal like I love cake—which is A LOT.

"What's up, Mom?" I replied sarcastically.

"I sure hope you're in bed; you have school bright and early." The tone in her voice was one of anticipation. There's something about the combination of first-day jitters mixed with optimism and freshly-ironed, crisp uniforms that excites her. Frankly, I don't get what the big deal is.

"I'm in the bed, Mom. Putting my journal away now."

"Did you take your medicine Charlie?"

"Of course I did, Mommy," I said as I reached over and grabbed my bottle of medicine off my nightstand. I popped two pills and washed them down with the bottle of water my mom keeps next to my bed. "Good night!" I yelled, switching off my lamp and snuggling into bed.

***

At 8:00 a.m., my alarm clock went off, alerting me that it was time to get ready for the first day of school. I jumped up in anticipation. I was so excited to wear the new clothes that my daddy had laid out the night before. They were ironed to a nice, clean crisp. I love the way my daddy irons my clothes. He always puts a crease in my pants, just like his. He comes over at least two nights out of the week to help me get ready for the next day. He would come over every night, but he said that his wife wants him to be home with her some nights to tuck her in—yuck!

The smell of French toast and smoked sausage knocked my nose into a frenzy.

Mommy cooks French toast for the first day of school every year. She is really into keeping traditions alive, or in her words, "Keeping things as normal as possible." I'm not sure why she's so insistent on maintaining traditions, but she's the best mother in the world so I'm sure she has good reasons.

"Rocky, come out of the bathroom already!" I screamed down the hall. Rocky spends two eternities in the bathroom every morning, and I always have to get ready while trying not to pass out from the scent of Japanese Blossom body wash.

"Put a sock in it," she responded, calmly, of course. Rocky never really yells at me like everyone else yells at their sisters. She treats me like a little baby and I hate it. Sometimes I wish that we could just fuss and fight like other girls do with their big sisters, but nope! Not Rocky! Finally making it to the shower, I decided to use a handful of Rocky's Orange Fusion body wash, and afterwards, I softly sprayed my face with her Orange Fusion perfume. *Kerplump!* The bottle fell to the floor. Glass and perfume splattered everywhere.

Rocky opened the bathroom door in a panic. "You alive in there Charlie?"

Stuttering, I responded, "Uh-uh, yes. I guess. I made a bit of a…mess."

Rocky stared at the floor and inhaled the scent of oranges from the perfume. "It's okay. I can always buy more," she said calmly.

"That's it? You're not mad?"

"Silly girl. Why would I be upset about something like this?"

I looked at my sister in shock, not knowing whether to be relieved or annoyed that she's so...perfect.

Finally, after long preparation for what seemed to be the most important day in a kid's life, we both flew down the stairs for breakfast and ran right into my mom holding up her iPhone, ready to take pictures.

"MOOOOOMMMMMMM!" Rocky and I yelled in torment. This was the part of the first day of school that we both HATED!

CHAPTER 4

"My Dear Lizzy"

Dear Journal,

What's a best friend? I'll tell you what it's not. It's not someone who leaves you on bad days and stops talking to you just because you ruffle their feathers a bit.

What's a best friend? I'll tell you what it is. It's someone who stays around and never leaves, even when you aren't really that likeable.

What's a best friend? I'll tell you what it's not. It's not someone who is only loyal to you when you're standing in front of them.

What's a best friend? I'll tell you what it is. It's someone who makes you feel lucky all day, every day, even when they aren't around.

What's a best friend? I'll tell you what it's not. It's not someone who lies to you and tells you your hair is pretty when it actually looks rotten.

What's a best friend? I'll tell you what it is. It's someone who is always honest, even when it makes them uncomfortable.
Love Always,
Charlie
P.S. Lizzy is everything a best friend could ever be, and more.

***

Lizzy and I met in the smelly halls of The Stafford School. I remember her first day at our school. She strutted into the classroom with so much confidence, wearing a black and white polka-dot dress; purple flats; and black glasses with a small, purple plastic bow stuck on the corner. Purple is my favorite color, so I couldn't take my eyes off of her as she strutted to her desk. *I want purple flats, and purple glasses, and a black and white polka-dot dress,* I thought to myself. Lizzy was perfect; the type of perfect that made you smile on the inside.

As she came closer, I noticed that she had on strawberry lip-gloss and smelled like pancake syrup and perfume. I rolled my eyes. *What ten-year-old wears lips gloss and perfume?*

Lizzy sat in the empty seat next to me and immediately turned to greet me. "Hi there!" she exclaimed. I turned my head, and before I could get the H in "Hello" out of my mouth, her beauty struck me like lightening. This was the most beautiful girl that I had ever seen in my life.

"HELLO?" she spoke again, and like an idiot, I just stared at her and mustered up a simple, "Hey."

"I'm Lizzy. What's your name?"

"Charlie," I whispered, wondering why she was talking so loudly.

"Charlie?" she asked, baffled. "Isn't that a boy's name?"

"No, it's my name!" I snapped back and turned around in my desk to face the front of the classroom.

Lizzy turned around and searched her book bag for her binder. When she pulled it out, her Michael Jackson notebook slid out. I picked it up and gasped.

"What?" she asked.

"You like Michael Jackson?" I responded abruptly. I'm sure she had assumed I was a weirdo by now.

"Doesn't everyone?" she responded.

"No! I thought I was the only ten-year old kid in the world who liked him."

"Hehe."

Lizzy told me that she had every Michael Jackson CD ever made, and in spite of my rudeness, she invited me over to listen to them after school. I knew then, that we were soul mates. I'm sure that she didn't know it yet, but I did. I didn't tell her because I didn't want to creep her out by being any weirder than I already was.

CHAPTER 5

"The First Day of School"

Dear Journal,

My mommy always tells me that change isn't always bad: "You're like an ocean, Charlie. Always moving, always shifting, sometimes calmly and sometimes forcefully." I'm not sure if I know exactly what she means, but I do know that my life changes...A LOT! Sometimes I feel like I will never overcome my illness. When I tell people I have lupus, they always stare at me in confusion, which is usually then followed by, "What is that?" It's SOOO annoying to have to ALWAYS explain something to people that you wish would just go away or just didn't even exist! I have, somehow, gotten used to a life where cold, white rooms have become this very familiar place for me. Sometimes, I read tall tales and watch funny movies to make passing the time a little easier, but the truth is, it never gets easier. I'm pretty sure that the biggest concern for the other kids in my grade doesn't include taking medicine every day. Oh, how I wish this was all just a dream and I could just wake up and only have to worry about whether someone is going to ask me to the school dance or not. Instead, I'm just relieved every time I actually wake up...

Love Always,
Charlie

***

Walking down the halls of The Stafford School of the Arts, I found myself listening to the familiar sounds of first-day-of-school excitement. Everyone was talking about what they did over the summer and what classes they signed up for this year. I looked around for my best friend to start a conversation of my own when I heard a loud voice screech down the main hall of The Stafford School.

"CHARLIEEEEE!"

I turned around and screamed as loud as I could. "My dear Lizzy Lizzy!"

All of the kids stared at me and Lizzy, but we didn't care.

"Oh, Charlie, when are you going to stop calling me that?" Lizzy asked, pulling me in for a hug. "You talk so grown up!"

"Whatever, Lizzy," I responded, sarcastically. "Show me your schedule!"

Lizzy pulled her schedule out of her pink, sequin book bag. "Here! Where's yours?"

I handed her mine, already annoyed because I knew she would have something smart to say. Sure enough, Lizzy exclaimed, "Creative writing! When did we get that here?

NUTRITION! Ok Charlie, is this a joke? Show me your REAL schedule!"

I let Lizzy get her hysterical laughs and her seemingly never-ending insults out of her system before responding with the biggest eye roll in the history of eye rolls. "Are you done?" I asked. I wasn't amused.

"Geez Charlie, lighten up why don't you? And yes, I'm done. *Hmph!*"

Amused by Lizzy's changed attitude, I responded, "Well, if you must know, my mom made the counselor put me in the nutrition class. She wants me to learn about my body so I can build better eating habits, blah blah blah… As for the writing class, well that was all me. Actually, I'm stoked about it. *HMPH!*"

Lizzy just stood there with a smile that went from ear to ear like the Cheshire Cat during my rant. Things like this are very typical for our relationship. I'm usually going on and on about something, taking life a bit too seriously, and Lizzy is usually smiling through it all, always finding something to laugh about. I guess you could say we're the perfect match! I smiled inside, reminiscing on our very awkward, but perfect friendship.

DING, DING, DING! At the sound of the bell, kids scattered everywhere saying quick goodbyes and see you laters as if they were not expecting it to ring. I told Lizzy I would meet her in class and I stood in the middle of the crowd, looking and listening to the kids as they ran to class, some still half asleep and others still boasting about their extravagant summer trips or rekindling old friendships. And then there was me, ready to go home because

I had a terrible headache and my legs were stiff! I bet the other kids didn't feel like their head was about to roll off of their neck any minute, BUT I headed to homeroom like everyone else.

I got to class just in time to slide into a desk behind Lizzy without the teacher seeing me.

"Yikes, you barely made it. What took you so long?" Lizzy said in her best teacher voice.

"I had to go to the restroom. I felt—well, I feel nauseous." I clinched my stomach in agony, but my stomach wasn't hurting.

Thomas, the class pest, who was sitting next to us, eavesdropping on our conversation, leaned over and whispered, "That time of the month, huh?"

"Yuck!" Lizzie yelled. "GET A LIFE THOMAS!"

The teacher swiveled around to face the class and turned her head abruptly to the left and then to the right, scanning the room. She lowered her glasses to the tip of her nose and gave the class the look that a mom gives her kid when she found their report card hidden in the junk drawer. Everyone just looked at her and smiled innocently as if nothing had happened.

When the teacher finally turned back to the board, Lizzy turned to me and asked, "What is it Charlie? IS IT that time of the month?"

"NO LIZZY!" I whispered loudly.

"Okay, okay, just checking…because you know I keep medicine in my—"

"LIZZY, STOP! YOU'RE MAKING IT WORSE!"

Lizzy started to ramble as she has the tendency to do when she finds herself in situations that she has no clue how to handle. This is just another way that we are complete opposites, because I always find a way to handle difficult situations.

Suddenly, I let out a long howl right in the middle of class. Everyone turned to look at me and all I could see were piercing eyes fixed on me like owls in the night. The pain in my legs was getting worse, it was getting harder and harder to breathe, and I was completely mortified! It's funny how after spending every waking moment in life breathing, you forget how important it actually is. The teacher didn't ask any questions. Instead, she walked right to the phone that hung next to the door and dialed my mom. I found myself slowly gasping for air and all those owl-eyed faces started to look fuzzy.

"Charlie!" Lizzy grabbed me by my shoulders and shook me back and forth. "CHARLIE!"

And then the shaking stopped…

CHAPTER 6

"Home From The Hospital"

Dear Journal,

The first day home from the hospital is always a drag. I always come home to a handmade "I'm glad you're back" pink, smiley-face card from Rocky; fresh white sheets; a spotless room that smells like those cinnamon bun candles that I love from my mommy; and a teddy bear from my daddy that usually sings a song or makes noise—a lot of noise. The card is here, the candles are here, sheets too, no bear though...not to mention this stack of homework. Uggghhhh. I cannot believe that I actually fainted in class and missed a week of school—the FIRST week! How mortifying!
Love Always,
Charlie

P.S. Lupus SUCKS!

***

I set my journal down on my nightstand and lay in my bed, deep in thought. I thought about everything that had happened in the past seven days. The first day of school, I got sick and had a lupus flare, missed an entire week of school, and now I have tons of homework to finish! The thing about lupus flares is that you never know when they will happen. That pretty much sums up my life; I just never know what the next day will bring.

A knock at the door interrupted my intense train of thought. I was actually a little relieved.

That's weird, I thought to myself. *Rocky usually just busts in. She must think I'm in a bad mood.* "Come in Rocky!"

"You feeling okay kiddo?" Rocky asked as she made her way into my room, closing the door behind her. "You've had a pretty rough week." Rocky's tone was a concerned one, somewhat somber.

"Yeah. I'm okay, I guess." I knew I was lying before the words even left my mouth.

"Well, you know I'm always here if you need me... You know Charlie, I really admire you."

I looked up at Rocky, baffled. "Seriously? Why? I would much rather be like you. Carefree, popular... You know, '*normal*.'"

I could tell that my reply threw Rocky off a bit, because she paused before responding. "Charlie, you are the bravest, smartest, most creative little girl I know. I don't know anybody else in the world like you. Do you know how many other little girls are out there going through what you're going through?"

Not needing much thought to answer such a question, I immediately replied, "Umm, none?"

"No, silly. Millions. Trust me, you're not alone, but I don't know if they're as strong as you, and what's so great about being normal anyway. Nobody is ever really normal. We all have our struggles, even me!" Rocky smiled.

Although I heard what Rocky was saying, I didn't quite understand. "I mean, I don't feel strong…or brave. I am pretty smart though!"

At that, we both burst into laughter.

"See Charlie, you CAN laugh through this. Laughing will make your days better. So, whenever you feel like crying, just laugh instead! That's what I do!" Rocky patted me on the knee and got up to leave.

"Hey, Rocky…" I said quickly.

Rocky stopped at the door and looked over her shoulder at me. "Yeah Charlie?"

"Thank you," I said, smiling awkwardly.

Rocky paused for a moment before she ran and jumped on top of me. She scruffed my already wild hair and we laughed. After catching her breath, Rocky responded, "That's what I'm here for, my little brave heart. Hey, why don't you audition for Dance Company with me? You haven't been involved in anything since last year. Come on, live a little! Besides, I've seen your moves, and you are AWESOME!"

Rocky always knew what to say. I beamed from ear to ear and replied, "That's okay, I'll just stick to what I know—writing."

Rocky sat up on the edge of my bed and looked me square in the eye. "Charlie, I really don't think you should stay cooped up in this room so much. Don't let fear be the guide in all of your decisions."

I rolled my eyes. "Bye, Rocky," I replied, sighing. Rocky headed for the door, looking back at me before walking out of view.

***

I walked out of my room, prepared to take a shower and wash my wild hair, which hadn't been washed since before my little "episode" at school. Right as I was about to step into the bathroom, I heard my mom and Rocky whispering downstairs in the kitchen. I tip-toed down the stairway just far enough to see Rocky and my mom.

Rocky had a very perturbed look on her face. "Mom can I ask you something?"

"Anything precious," Mom responded. My mom absolutely loves when we talk to her.

"I know Charlie is kind of, well, sick and all, but Dance Company auditions are in two weeks, and I wasn't going to even ask because Charlie is, well, sick and all, but I really want to do this more than anything else! I'm really good and I know I would make it—"

Growing impatient, Mom said firmly, "Spit it out Roberta! What is it?"

Rocky took a breath so deep you would have thought she was about to announce that she was running for President of the United States. Finally, she said, "Could I possibly have six hundred dollars for Dance Company auditions? I'll do whatever! I'll clean up; I'll wash the car; I'll even walk the dog! Please, please, pleaseeeeee Mom!" Rocky pleaded on and on like this for at least two more minutes before Mom finally cut her off.

"Rocky, STOP! I get it, and we don't even have a dog."

Mom took a deep sigh.

"Sweetie, I am so proud of you for wanting to do this, and you are such an awesome big sister for always thinking about Charlie, but with all of Charlie's medical bills; prescriptions; and you guys' tuition, I just..."

Rocky hung her head wistfully. *Poor Rocky*, I thought. *Always having to sacrifice for me.*

My mom looked so defeated. When Rocky seemed to notice this, she lifted her head and said, "It's okay, Mom. I get it. Maybe next time." Although she was talking to my mom, she sounded more like she was trying to convince herself. Her voice gave away her disappointment as she forced a slight smirk.

My mom didn't say a word. Rocky had been talking about auditioning for one of the leading spots in Dance Company for years. She always said that she would be the first ninth grader to audition for it at our school. Most girls don't make it to the forefront of Dance Company until they're eleventh graders, but Rocky is good! I've never seen anyone dance quite like her. We both go to a fancy arts school that apparently costs a lot of money, but Rocky and I have scholarships, so my mom only has to pay a small amount. Still, she has to pay for so many other things since she mostly takes care of us by herself.

I have to figure something out. Rocky deserves this more than anything, and it's my fault she can't have it. Suddenly, a light bulb went off in my head, and before I knew it, I was heading back up the stairs to call my dad.

Daddy has a lot of money. He just bought a fancy, red convertible car. I just know he would have the money to pay for Rocky to go after her dream! Filled with excitement, I picked up the phone and dialed my dad's home number. *Ring…ring…ring.* The phone rang for about forty-five seconds. There was no answer, so I dialed him again…and again…and again. *That's odd, Daddy always answers the phone for me*, I thought. I decided I would try once more. This time he picked up.

"Charlie! Baby girl! Are you okay?" he answered in a panic.

Snickering, I replied, "I'm cool Daddy. Are you okay? Why are you screaming?"

"Because you called me three times! Usually when someone calls that much, there's an emergency. I figured either someone died or someone ate your cheese puffs!"

We both laughed hysterically. Daddy knows I love my cheese puffs. His laughter quickly faded into silence.

"Daddy are you there?" I asked.

"I'm here baby girl. I just miss you—you and Rocky—but what's up?" he replied somberly.

"I'm glad you asked. Rocky wants to audition for one of the leading spots in Dance Company, but Mommy doesn't have the money, and, well, it costs six hundred dollars. Since Mommy's paying our tuition and my medical bills, I figured, you know, you could give her the money, or whatever…maybe?" Worried that I was starting to ramble like Lizzy when she's faced with a difficult situation, I decided to stop talking and wait for a reply.

Daddy released a deep sigh. "Why couldn't she call and ask me herself? Did she put you up to this? And for the record, I do help your mom with your tuition AND your medical bills." With every word, my dad's voice thickened.

"DAD! That's not the point! She is always sacrificing for us and she shouldn't have to, Dad. She just shouldn't! I mean, you didn't even bring me a teddy bear when I got out of the hospital! Do you even care anymore, Dad? DO YOU?" Without waiting for a reply, I hung up the phone, infuriated, but at the same time, shocked. I couldn't believe that I just spoke to my dad that way. *Yikes, Charlie, I thought to myself.* He used to be the best Daddy ever. I can remember when he and Mommy first got divorced, he would come over every night, give me a bath, read me a bed time story, and tuck me in. It was as if he had never left. My head immediately begin to fill with crummy thoughts, so I pulled out my headphones, hoping to drown them out.

CHAPTER 7

"The Audition"

Dear Journal,

"Daddy, do you love me?"
"Yes."
"How do you know?"
"How do I know?"
"Yes, how do you know?"
"I know.
Because grass is green and flowers grow,
Because the winds blow, and so does snow.
Because the sun sets and the moon rises,
Because the world comes in different shapes and sizes.
Because birds have wings and people have feet,
Because water is wet, and sugar is sweet.
You ask do I love you and how do I know,
Because you are you, and God intended that it be so."

Love Always,
Charlie

P.S. A daddy's love grows like a tree,
especially my daddy. ☺

I had written this poem about my daddy a few years ago. Things have changed a lot since then.

***

Rocky has been running around the house all morning, making way too much noise. Her Dance Company auditions are today and she is on pins and needles. I don't know who paid for them and I don't really care, I'm just glad to see my sister get the chance to live out her dream! I get to go watch the auditions with Mommy. I'm not a great dancer, so I live that part of life vicariously through my sister and the other dancers at my school.

"Girls! We have to go!" Mom shouts up the stairs. "Rocky, eat something quick! Charlie, take your meds—" Mom stopped right in her tracks.

"What is it, Mommy? Nothing's wrong, right?" I asked.

"Charlie... I just remembered it's the fourth week of the month."

"So?" I replied.

"So, you have a doctor's appointment today. SHUCKS! I'm going to have to see if Ms. Bittersnap can take Rocky to her audition."

Rocky entered the room just as Mom was finishing her sentence. "Mom! You can't send me with her!" she shouted. "I really want you to be there. I need you. Like, really need you."

The longing in Rocky's voice was so obvious. There was no way I was going to ruin this day for Rocky. I turned to Mom and looked at her with pleading eyes. "I can just go next week Mom. I'm fine, really! I feel great! Let's just take Rocky, please. I want to!" I could tell that my mom was not convinced.

"Charlie, please. This is more impor—" She stopped herself before she uttered the words that she always promised herself she wouldn't say.

"More important?" Rocky interrupted. "Is that what you were going to say Mom? I understand. I get it, and it's really okay." Rocky pushed her breakfast away, wiped her hands on a napkin, and got up from the table.

"No sweetie, I didn't mean it like that. It's just that Charlie needs me, and Ms. Bittersnap wouldn't possibly know what questions to ask the doctor."

Rocky tucked her chair under the dining room table. "I said it's okay Mom," Rocky said, seeming to maintain her calm demeanor. "I know Charlie needs you."

I knew she didn't mean it. Deep down, Rocky was hurting.

"I'll take her."

Everyone looked toward the door in surprise, looking to see who had just jumped into our conversation. We all grew tense as a figure made its way around the corner.

"Daddyyyyy!" Rocky and I yelled as the formally ominous figure made its way into the kitchen.

"Hey, my sweet girls," Dad said. Then he turned to me, winked, and mouthed the words "I'm sorry."

I smiled and gave Dad a hug. I looked over his shoulder at my mom. She didn't look too happy, but she pretended not to be phased by Daddy's unexpected visit.

"Alright ladies," she announced, "Dad will take Charlie to the doctor and I will take Rocky to her audition. Now let's go!"

As we headed toward the door, I saw Mom whisper something to Dad that made him roll his eyes, but I pretended that I didn't notice and pranced out of the door blissfully!

■■■

I hopped in Daddy's new red car. It was one the most beautiful cars that I'd ever seen. "Nice wheels, Dad!" I commented.

Dad chuckled. "Thanks little woman. So how's your mom?"

"That's an odd question, but she's fine I guess. How's your mom?"

He laughed once again. "You're on a roll today aren't you? I just wanted to know. She seems stressed."

I paused for a minute, attempting to do something I never do: think before I speak. Finally, I said, "Well, Dad, I think you stress her out. I think she gets tired of taking care of me sometimes and you not being around to help is hard on her."

Suddenly, Daddy looked as if he was going to cry. "Charlie, don't you ever say that again. We could never get tired of you. What's there to get tired of? You're the best daughter anyone could ask for!"

"Well Dad, you're not with me every day. Mom is just overwhelmed, and maybe she just needs a break. Yeah, that's it! She needs a vacation!"

"You just have all the answers, don't you baby girl? You always were a wise one."

"Yes, Dad. I am a realist."

"Okay, that's enough of the serious talk. How about lunch after your appointment, just you and me?"

"Music to my ears!" I replied, excited for the day that lay ahead.

***

As Daddy and I approached Doctor Bruzar's office, I started to feel my heart beat louder and faster in my chest. I've been to at least a gazillion doctor's appointments and I still get anxious at each one as if it's the first time. Daddy signed me in and we sat down in the waiting area. The room felt as if it was negative three degrees and the smell of latex gloves and metal gave me a queasy feeling. Many of the areas that were designed for kids were very colorful and artistic, but the rheumatology area, which is where all of the kids like me go, is pretty much all blue. There are blue chairs and blue walls, blue pens and blue tables—even the nurses wear blue!

"Charlie Bradshaw!" Nurse Mildred called enthusiastically, as if my name had been pulled for a raffle or something. I could never understand how anyone could be so enthusiastic at a time like this. I was feeling a lot of things, but enthusiastic sure wasn't one of them. "Charlie Bradshaw?" she called again. "Is Charlie here?"

"I'm here, I'm here, Nurse Mildred!" I finally replied.

"There she is!" She reached out to give me one of those big hugs that I hate. The ones where she pulls me into her bosom, kisses me a million times, and leaves my face stained with orange lipstick. "How are you, Ms. Charlie Bradshaw?" Nurse Mildred calls all of the kids by their first and last names. Mom says it's because she's old and it helps her to remember everyone.

"I'm awesome, Nurse Mildred," I replied, attempting to match her enthusiasm. "You?"

"You know me! If you're good, I'm good. Now I'm going to need a little yellow water and red juice from you." This is Nurse Mildred's way of saying that I need to pee in a cup and get my blood drawn. I nodded and I followed her to the lab so she could draw my blood.

Nurse Mildred placed a handful of tubes with ridged yellow tops on the table and prepared to draw my blood. Geez, there were at least five, six, seven…twenty tubes that needed to be filled with blood—MY blood! She looked at me, smiled, and softly whispered, "Close your eyes Charlie." Nurse Mildred always finds a way to distract me while she's taking my vitals and drawing blood, just in case my numbers are low. I guess she thinks I'd freak out. If that's the reason, she's not wrong.

I scooted back in the cold, blue chair, leaned my head against it, and closed my eyes. I felt a tiny prick, and then another, and then another. After the first three pricks, the rest didn't feel so tiny anymore. After what seemed like forever, I opened one eye to peek at Nurse Mildred. As soon as I looked down at my arm, she said, "There it is! I'm sorry sweetheart, these veins weren't giving up any blood today, but we are good now!" I smiled weakly and lay back again.

As Nurse Mildred labeled and organized the freshly drawn vials of blood, I began to count the pieces of fruit on the wallpaper. By the time I had gotten to eighty-six, Nurse Mildred knocked me out of my daze. "Alrighty little lady!" she exclaimed. "Head on to the restroom, bring me my yellow water, and then head to room fourteen. Dr. Bruzar will see you shortly."

After following Nurse Mildred's instructions, I entered room fourteen and hopped onto the exam table. My dad was already in the room, sitting in the chair designated for an extra person. As I looked around the room at the light brown walls and the computer with the doctor's chair, I noticed that my dad looked nervous; as if he was the one we were here for. Concerned, I asked, "You okay, Daddy? Dad... DAD!"

After the last holler, Dad snapped out of his daze. "YES, I'm here! What's up?" he replied frantically.

"Talk to me, Dad. When Mom brings me, she always talks to me, so you have to talk to me...about anything." My voice trailed off as

I sat on the cold exam table twiddling my thumbs. Daddy gazed up at the ceiling as if he were looking for words to fall out of the sky. It was obvious that he didn't know what to say and I didn't know what to say either, so we both just sat in silence for at least fifteen minutes. It was taking longer than usual.

"Good morning!" Dr. Bruzar burst through the door, jolly and loud as usual. Dad and I perked up, thankful that the awkward silence had ended. "How are you, Ms. Charlie?" Dr. Bruzar asked.

I wanted to say, "I'm confused, my head hurts, I'm tired, my dad is annoying, I can't keep any food down, and I wish someone would ask me to the seventh grade dance," but all I could muster up was, "Fine, just fine."

"Well Charlie, your mom called me a few minutes before you and your dad arrived. She told me about the complications you've been having."

"Complications?" Dad interrupted.

"Yes, I assumed you were aware," Dr. Bruzar said sarcastically.

It seemed as though Dad had heard the sarcasm in Dr. Bruzar's voice just as well as I had. Dad frowned and quickly murmured, "Go on..."

Dr. Bruzar rolled his tiny, black stool across the room and sat down directly in front of me so our eyes could meet. "Charlie, do you mind stepping outside with Nurse Mildred? She could use your help tidying up the kids' area."

I gave him a blank stare. *How old does he think I am!* I thought. "In other words, you want me to leave the room so you can talk to my dad," I responded bitterly. "It's cool. I get it. I'm not a baby, ya know."

Dad and Mr. Bruzar both chuckled.

I hopped off of the table and made my way back to the waiting area.

***

    I sat in the waiting room in deep thought while watching a woman chase her son around. I thought about what Dr. Bruzar could have been telling my dad. *It's bad. I know it's bad. Or maybe it's good! Maybe they want to surprise me with good news! Nah, I know it's bad.* Suddenly, my cell phone vibrated. My phone never rings unless it's Mommy or Rocky. The screen read "Rocky" and above her name was a picture of her smiling from ear to ear. Rocky must have put it there herself.

Rocky always finds a way to make

everyone's day better, even when she's not

around. I laughed to myself and opened the

text she sent. It read:

> Hey my little brave heart! I just wanted you to know that I'm thinking of you. Mom and I prayed for you on the way to my audition. I know I tell you all the time, but you are my biggest inspiration and there is NOTHING you can't handle! XOXO

Just like that, all of my worry went away. Rocky

always tells me how brave I am. I started to

think about why she always chooses the word

"brave." Not strong, not courageous, but

BRAVE.

Finally, I saw my dad and Dr. Bruzar

standing at the door that connected the waiting

room to the patient care area. They shook

hands and Dad started shaking his head, which meant that something was wrong.

"You ready to go and grab some lunch baby girl?" my dad asked once he was within talking distance.

I guess he wasn't ready to tell me whatever he and Dr. Bruzar had talked about, so I just played along. "Yep! Pizza?" I replied, pretending to be excited.

"Pizza it is!"

CHAPTER 8

"Bad News"

Dear Journal,

So, what does it mean to be brave? Why is it so hard for me to admit that small and trivial things hurt me, and when I overcome them, that's considered an act of bravery? I am absolutely terrified of praying aloud, so every time it's my turn to say grace, I have to round up as much courage as possible to perform this very simple act that others seem to find so easy. That's a form of bravery, I suppose. I think in order for a person to be considered truly brave, they have to have a brave heart. I guess that's why Rocky always tells me that I don't give myself enough credit. I wake up every day and face my scars—scars that I didn't bring upon myself. I face lupus every day, and I do so courageously! I hate being asked, "What's wrong." I don't need anyone to feel bad for me. Life hasn't always

played fair with me, but I just have to
keep on going with the hand that I've
been dealt...
Love Always,
Charlie
P.S. I guess my heart IS one of the
bravest. ☺

***

"Dialysis?" I uttered. "What does that even

mean?" After my dad and I had gotten back

home from lunch, Mom, Dad, and Rocky sat

me down to talk about what Dr. Bruzar told my

dad. Basically, my body sucks and it wasn't

functioning the way that it should be.

Mom took a deep sigh. "Well sweetie,

dialysis is just a precaution Dr. Bruzar wants to

take so that he can clean all of the bad stuff out

of your body." She was trying so hard to

explain this "dialysis" business to me, but I still didn't quite understand.

"So let me get this straight. My kidneys aren't working right, so I have to go through some treatments so that they will work again? If they aren't working, why can't I just get new ones?"

Mom turned to Dad and gave him a "your turn" look. My dad turned to me and said softly, "Well baby girl, apparently there are thousands of other people in the world that are just like you and they need kidneys too, so what the doctors do is, they put you on a list. When it's your turn, they will call us and you will get a new one."

Filled with relief, I said, "Oh! Well we can just wait then! *Whew!* I thought there was no way for me to get one." Judging by Mom and Dad's flustered faces, I was wrong. "No?" I said. "There's more?"

It looked as if Mommy was about to shed a tear. "Sweetie…" She paused for a second. "Sweetie, you don't exactly have that kind of time. You see, we can't really afford to wait, so we have to begin the treatment now, which is where the dialysis comes in. It will only be three times a week and it should only last a couple of hours. That's it! And I will be there every step of the way."

Mom reached over and rested her hand on my knee. My eyes began to swell and I was fighting to hold back tears. I couldn't let her see me cry. Not about this. "Okay. Okay Mom… Well, I guess I have to do what I have to do." I cleared my throat and took a deep breath. It was getting more and more difficult to hold back my tears. "May I be excused?"

Before my mom could answer, I ran upstairs to my room, locked the door, and opened my journal. I couldn't find a pen so I grabbed a crayon off of my desk.

Dear Journal,

WHY ME? WHY ME? WHY ME? WHY ME?

P.S. WHY ME?

Not wanting to think about dialysis or kidneys or anything else, I closed my journal, climbed into bed, and went to sleep.

CHAPTER 9

"Lizzy To The Rescue"

I was awakened by a knock at the door, and before I could even sit up, someone flung the door open, ran into my room, jumped into my bed, and landed right beside me. I sat up frantically and looked over to see Lizzy wearing a black leotard, gray sweatpants, a Michael Jackson bandana, and black dance sneakers. "It's the cheer up police to the rescue!" Lizzy exclaimed.

We both laughed.

"My dear Lizzy," I said, "did my mom call you? Because I'm fine, really!"

Lizzy pretended to have no idea what I was talking about. "I can't just want to see your beautiful, round face? Geez, Charlie! I was just leaving Junior Dance Company auditions and I really wanted to see you!"

I wasn't buying it. "Well here's my face. See it?" I asked sarcastically, leaning toward Lizzy obnoxiously.

Lizzy ignored my attempts to get her to leave me alone.

"No offense Lizzy, but I just want to sleep. Today hasn't been that great, ya know?" I plopped back down on my pillow, hoping that would be enough to get Lizzy to go back home.

Lizzy replied, "Well go to sleep then! I'll just watch T.V." She grabbed the remote to my T.V. and turned to the music video channel.

I closed my eyes and smiled. *Lizzy is a true friend.*

CHAPTER 10

"Day One"

"Charlie! Charlie, wake up! We need to be leaving in the next thirty minutes."

I turned over and looked at the digital clock on my dresser, which read 4:13 a.m. *Seriously, Mom!* I thought to myself.

Today is the first day of my dialysis treatments and I am scared out of my mind. Mom said it doesn't hurt and I will only have to do it until my kidneys get better.

Mom laid my clothes out for me the night before, which was strange. After getting ready, I walked down to the kitchen to find that my mom had also prepared a plate of breakfast for me: two scrambled eggs, a piece of turkey bacon, one slice of jelly wheat toast, and bottled water. I tried to eat as much as I could without vomiting.

I was more nervous than I had ever been in my life. My hands were trembling and I could barely feel my legs. I began to hum the tune to "Rock & Roll All Nite" in my head, hoping that my nerves would subside.

***

As we pulled up to the clinic, Mom turned to me and said, "I will be right next to you."

Rocky added, "Yeah, Charlie! Me too." Rocky had decided to ride with us because she thought it would make me feel better, and she was right!

As we walked into the clinic, I clinched my fists tight, feeling the sweat build up in my palms. As soon as we entered the building, a nurse escorted me to the back. She turned and asked my mom if she was coming. Mommy looked at me, for an answer, I guess. "I'll be okay," I told her as I forced myself to smile.

"Of course she will!" Rocky shouted. "She's the bravest of them all!"

Mom seemed to relax a little. Unfortunately, the truth was that I wasn't okay, but if me pretending that I am makes my mom feel better, then so be it.

I stepped into a big, white room. It was freezing and all I could hear was a low buzzing sound. The nurse sat me down in a large, white chair that, in any other situation, I may have considered comfortable. Grabbing the arms of the chair in terror, I looked to my left and noticed a big, grey machine with a huge screen on it. It had a red and blue button and what seemed like a hundred switches. The nurse tapped my arm and softly murmured,

"Now this is only going to hurt for a little while, pinky promise."

I nodded my head, leaned back, and closed my eyes. I felt the first prick, but it wasn't like the pricks I usually feel when I get my blood drawn. I looked down to find the nurse inserting a huge needle into my arm. I quickly shut my eyes, attempting to erase that nerve-wracking image from my mind. I guess the nurse saw the tears falling from the corners of my eyes, because she began to rub my arm. "You're doing great, Charlie," she said. "Just one more."

She slid the second needle into my arm. The pain was unbearable and I really didn't feel like being brave anymore, but I just keep my eyes closed and waited for the pain to go away. Once the needle was completely inserted, I heard the nurse say, "All done, Charlie. You were amazing! Just keep your eyes closed and get some rest."

I kept my eyes closed even as she spoke to me, not intending to open them for any reason.

CHAPTER 11

"Everyone Can Fly"

"Hey little girl." I felt a slight peck on my cold cheek. "Wake up, little girl! Little girl! LITTLE GIRL CAN YOU HEAR ME?"

I slowly opened my eyes only to find a little bird sitting on my forehead. "Aaaahhhhhhhh! Nurse, nurse, help me!" I screamed frantically.

"Hush up all that fussing, little girl. Haven't you ever seen a bird before?"

I quickly jumped to my feet. As I scanned the room, I noticed that there was no room! Only a swarm of colorful birds flying in a circular motion around me. *How did I end up in a forest?* I thought to myself.

The bird jumped off of my forehead down to the palm of my sweaty hand. I stared at the bird in disbelief. It was odd, beautiful to say the least. I wasn't sure what type of bird it was. It looked like a pigeon. It had big feathers like a peacock, but they were beautifully and brightly colored like a parrot's. "Are you…real?" I asked the bird, still in total disbelief that I was actually talking to a bird.

The bird responded, "The question is, are YOU real? Of course I'M real! Feel my feathers! Go on, feel 'em!"

I gave the bird a hard poke.

"Whoa!" The bird screamed. "I said feel, not kill!"

"Sorry…" I murmured. "Umm, where am I? Who are you? Why do you TALK?" I was still so confused.

"One question at a time!" The bird squawked. "Well my dear, you're in the Great Kaleidoscope Forest! This is my nest! Benji Bird is the name! Yours?"

"Charlie. I think." Thinking. Something I was finding extremely hard to do when so many talking birds surrounded me. "To be honest Mr. Bird, I'm not too sure about anything right now."

"That's MISSES Bird, little girl! I mean, Charlie." The bird snapped back.

"Oh! My apologies, it's just that Benji is sort of a boy's name, ya know?"

Benji cut her eyes at me and blurted out, "And so is Charlie! I'm no ordinary bird, ya know, so I don't need no ordinary name! *Hmph!*"

Point taken, I thought.

"Now that we've gotten that out of the way, you ready to fly little girl?"

I jumped back a step. "Fly! No one said anything about flying! I'm just here to get a little procedure, that's it! No flying over here! Nope, nope, nope!" I turned around to walk away and realized that I had NO IDEA where I was going!

Benji trailed behind me. "Well what did you come here for? Most of the kiddies that come here come ready to face their fears and fly! And what kind of procedure you talkin' 'bout? You okay little girl? You talkin' crazy now!"

"Is this bird crazy!" I whispered to myself.

"No, I'm not crazy! You the crazy one, talkin' 'bout you can't fly. That's crazy talk right there! Everybody can fly, they just don't know it yet. Now come on little girl! I'm gonna help you at first and then it's up to you! You ready?"

"NO!" I screamed.

"GOOD! Let's go then!" Benji replied, completely ignoring my plea.

"I said no, Benji!" I continued to scream as Benji flew around me in circles, pecking at me. She pecked at my legs, then my arms, then my head. *What is she doing?* I thought. "Benji, I can't fly! I'm just a girl, NOT a bird. Benji! BENJI!"

Suddenly, I was in the air. I looked down to find my feet dangling far above the floor. I started to swing them back and forth. Then, I flapped my arms up and down, up and down. "I can't believe my eyes!" I shouted. "I'm flying!"

"Yep, ya sure are!" Benji replied. "Now keep your eyes on me and let's go!"

I had never felt so free before! Benji and I flew over snow-capped mountains, wet grasslands, a volcano, and even a farm of unicorns! After circling the entire land, we finally returned to Benji's nest, where there were three other birds just like her! Since I didn't know what type of birds they were, I figured I would just call them Benjis!

"See!" Benji said. "Now, don't you ever forget this! Once you've had a little taste of the sky, the ground isn't as comfy as it was before, so keep your eyes to the sky little girl. I've got to get you back home. Close your eyes little girl!"

I closed my eyes, and I before I knew it, I was asleep.

CHAPTER 12

"My Time To Fly"

I slowly opened my eyes and found myself back in the white dialysis room. I looked over to find my mom and Rocky in deep conversation with one another. Looking down, I noticed that the needles that were once in my arm had been replaced by a big, white bandage.

I let out a huge yawn and stretched. Mom and Rocky immediately turned their attention to me. Mom spoke first. "Welcome back, sleepy head. Your treatment was over a while ago, but you were sleeping so soundly that we decided to let you rest."

Glancing at the clock on the wall, I noticed that it was almost nine o'clock. Panicked, I shouted, "We have to get to school! We're late!"

Mom smiled. "Only if you're feeling up to it. I was just going to drop Rocky off, and then you and I could hang together the rest of the day."

"I think I'm fine, Mom. Now, can we get to school?" I couldn't wait to see Lizzy so I could tell her about my dream!

Mom shifted positions in her chair. "I don't know, Charlie... Your day has been quite an eventful one already. I want you to get used to the treatments first. Don't feel like you have to force yourself to do anything. You don't have anything to prove, you know that right?" Mom seemed really nervous about me going to school.

"Mom! I'm fine! I promise! How am I ever going to fly if you don't allow me to spread my wings?"

"Are you okay, Charlie?" Rocky asked. "What's up with the 'I'm every woman' quotes?"

I ignored her and let out one of my signature eye rolls. "Nothing. Can we just blow this joint and go to school now?"

Rocky laughed. "Whoa, Charlie! Look at you. A 'grown woman' quote, and now a 'grown woman' eye roll! Go ahead then, girl! Well, mom, if Charlie can be brave enough to go to school with the day she's had, I think you can be brave enough to let her," Rocky snapped and moved her head from side to side.

Everyone laughed and Mom seemed to relax a little, and before we knew it, she had burst into tears! Rocky and I stood still and just looked at each other. Neither of us knew what to do or what to say. Rocky began to caress mom's back, so I followed suit and stroked her soft black hair. Mom gave us an awkward look as if she was wincing, "These are not sad tears, you two are just the best gift I could have ever received. Charlie, you teach me so much everyday about being persistent and never giving up. Rocky, your patience and love for your sister inspires me so much," mom sniffled and wiped her face about three times, she then took a deep breath, "Okay, then!" she said. "Let's go!"

We left the clinic and Mom drove Rocky and me to school. During the car ride, I pulled my journal out of my book bag and wrote:

Dear Journal,
"Everyone Can Fly, They Just Don't Know It Yet!"
Can they? Can I? I've never felt so free! The sky made me feel invincible. I can't even imagine feeling that way every day. I've been afraid for so long that I don't remember what it feels like to "fly" without reservation. Although it was just a

dream, I wish I could be that very brave girl: soaring through the air, not even thinking about the ground, not afraid of falling. I want to fly high, above the world, above the scars, above my insecurities. But what if my wings break in mid-air? But what if they don't?
Love Always,
Charlie

P.S. But what if they don't...

Meet The Author!

Tommia M. Brookins is the author of P.S. Charlie, Memoirs of A Little Brave Girl With A Big Brave Heart. As an educator, wife, lupus survivor, lupus advocate, and mentor, she's learned the real meaning of bravery and humanity. She has used this unfortunate happening as a stepping-stone to help little girls everywhere discover the bravery inside of them! She is the founder of BraveHeart University and The Brave Girls Book Club, which is a community of brave individuals who uplift and encourage one another to  walk in the bravery that lies in every heart! If she could use one word to describe herself, it would be BRAVE of course! Brookins states, "I have not always been this very brave woman. There was a time when I couldn't even fathom winning, which is why BraveHeart University means the world to me. I have made it my mission to not only remind myself that I am not to be underestimated, but to remind YOU!"

Find Tommia Brookins and the Brave Girls Book Club at Braveheartuniversity.org. I LIVE BRAVE accessories and P.S.Charlie are also for sale on Braveheartuniversity.org. For contact, bookings, or just a simple word of encouragement, email tommiabrookins@gmail.com

DAILY AFFIRMATIONS FOR:

_____

(Your Name Here)

I AM GOOD

I AM SPECIAL

I AM AN EXAMPLE

I AM A HARDWORKER

I AM A LEADER

I AM AN INSPIRATION

I AM STRONG

I DESERVE THE BEST

I AM RARE

I AM A SUCCESS

I AM GIFTED

I AM PURPOSED

I AM A QUEEN/KING

I AM BRAVE & MY HEART IS BRAVE!

Feel free to tear this page out and place it on your mirror so that everyday you will be reminded to BE YOU and all that you are called to be!

www.ingramcontent.com/pod-product-compliance
Lightning Source LLC
Chambersburg PA
CBHW071008280626
47160CB00015B/2067